Kit the Cat

Illustrated by
Maddy McClellan

This book is to be returned on or before the last date stamped below

1 3 MAY 2016   − 5 SEP 2018
− 1 SEP 2016   1 7 OCT 2018
0 7 OCT 2016
1 2 OCT 2016
2 4 MAR 20
1 5 APR 2017
1 5 DEC 2017

Please return on or before the latest date above.
You can renew online at www.kent.gov.uk/libs
or by phone 08458 247 200

17 SEP 2015   − 8 MAR 2019
                − 8 MAR 2019
1 4 MAY 2014

CHARTER MARK
CUSTOMER SERVICE EXCELLENCE

Kent
County
Council

Libraries & Archives

D0241477

Kit the Cat
cleaned and preened
on the long,
lush lawn.

Flash the Fish
flipped and flopped
in the pretty,
paved pond.

Kit the Cat
sat and spat
as Flash the Fish
leapt and lapped.

Kit the Cat scowled and prowled towards the pretty, paved pond.

Flash the **Fish**
Smirked and lurked in the deep,
dark depths.

Kit the Cat
pawed and clawed
at the deep, **dark** depths

and **Flash** the **Fish**
jeered and jumped.

Kit the Cat missed and **hissed.**

Flash the Fish splashed and sploshed.

then Kit the Cat
lunged and plunged,
flipping Flash the Fish
out of the pretty, paved pond.

Dig the Dog
appeared and
jeered...

...and leapt
the great
garden gate.

Kit the Cat
licked her lips.

Flash the Fish
flopped and flapped
on the lush, green grass.

Dig the Dog
growled and
howled.

Kit the Cat
licked and picked up
Flash the Fish
then span and ran
through the clackety
cat flap.

Dig the **Dog**
pushed and pounded
on the **clackety**
cat flap.

Kit the **Cat**
dropped the floundering fish
into the **big**, blue bowl.

Dig the Dog
squished and squeezed
through the **clackety** cat flap.

Kit the Cat
screeched and
scratched

and Dig the Dog
gnarled and snarled.

Kit the **Cat**
sulked and skulked
out of the **clackety**
cat flap.

Dig the Dog grabbed and dragged the **big**, blue bowl through the **clackety** cat flap.

across the **long**, lush lawn
to the pretty,
paved pond.

...and **Flash** the **Fish** slithered and slid into the **deep**, **dark** depths.

For joe, with love.

A.M.

For Inigo Tiger and Lee,
Cameron and Rowan

M.M.

First published in 2008
by Meadowside Children's Books
185 Fleet Street London EC4A 2HS
www.meadowsidebooks.com

Text © Alison Maloney 2008
Illustrations © Maddy McClellan 2008
The rights of Alison Maloney and Maddy McClellan
to be identified as the author and illustrator
have been asserted by them in accordance with
the Copyright, Designs and Patents Act, 1988

A CIP catalogue record for this book is available
from the British Library

10 9 8 7 6 5 4 3 2 1
Printed in Indonesia